KITTEN AND CAT STORIES

TO READ ALOUD

Compiled by OSCAR WEIGLE
Illustrated by ELIZABETH DAUBER

WONDER BOOKS • NEW YORK

ACKNOWLEDGMENTS

Grateful acknowledgment and thanks are extended to the following sources for stories appearing in this book:

"Copy Cat" and "Juliet's Special Valentine," by Molly C. Rodman, copyright 1953, 1954 by Quality Magazines, Inc. (These stories first appeared in *Piggity's Magazine*, a subsidiary of the publishers of *Parents' Magazine*.)

"The Adventures of Boots," by Gail Stephenson, copyright 1955 by Humpty Dumpty, Inc. (This story first appeared in *Humpty Dumpty's Magazine for Little Children*, a subsidiary of the publishers of *Parents' Magazine*.)

CONTENTS

Note to Parents

One of the most gratifying ways of bringing the precious feeling of closeness to your family is sharing the joys of reading with your children. More and more parents are discovering the pleasures of a daily Storytime Hour . . . a time for reading aloud to young children, helping them develop a lifetime love of books, stimulating their imagination, enriching their vocabularies, and teaching them fascinating facts about the world around them.

Read-Aloud books are especially planned for the small child who loves to listen to a story—and also for the beginning reader who is proud of his new talent and wants to show it off for your approval.

You will enjoy reading these stories to your young children. You will enjoy them perhaps even more when your child proudly reads the stories to you.

HOW MISS TABITHA CAT TAUGHT SCHOOL

By EDMUND VANCE COOKE

IN MALTESE STREET, in the city of Kitty-polis, there lived an elderly maidencat who thought she would teach school. So she hung out a sign:

MISS TABITHA CAT
MOUSE KINDERGARTEN
NUMBERS A SPECIALTY

For a long time the many mouse families of the neighborhood would have nothing to do with her, but one day she received a card bearing the name:

Mrs. Roberta De House-Mouse
Hole-in-the-wall No. 4
Attica Apartments

Miss Tabitha received Mrs. De House-Mouse most graciously, although there was a suspicious licking of her lips whenever her visitor turned her head to look at the pictures on the walls.

"I have ten children, my dear Miss Cat," said the visitor, "and they are quite a trial to me at times."

"After a term with me," purred Miss Cat softly, "I think I can assure you they will never trouble you again." (Now what do you suppose that she meant by that?)

"Numbers is my specialty," continued Miss Cat, modestly. "I have a new system which gives remarkable results."

So the next morning the ten little De House-Mouses started school with Miss Tabitha Cat. They were Whiskerando, White-Tooth, Bright-Eyes, Long-Tail, Soft-Foot, Fatness, Spryness, Cuteness, Sleekness and Blackieback. Miss Cat's large green eyes shone with delight to look at them.

"My dear children," she began, "your first day's lesson is in addition, sometimes known as 'disguised subtraction.' You, my dear Whiskerando, White-Tooth, Long-Tail, Bright-Eyes and Soft-Foot, are in one class, and you, my sweet Fatness, Spryness, Cuteness, Sleekness and Blackieback, are in another. You will observe that there are five in the first class and four in the second class."

"Please, teacher," said Blackieback, sitting up and counting his toes rapidly.

"Don't interrupt," said Miss Cat sharply. "Listen to the lesson. Five in one class and four in the other are ten. Now, how many are five and four?"

"Five and four are ten! Five and four are ten!" repeated the silly mice—all but Blackieback.

"Blackieback must go into the closet and remain there for the rest of the day," said Miss Cat severely. So poor Blackieback was put in the closet.

When the time came for school to let out, Miss Cat said, "Now, my dears, we always call the roll at dismissal, and we call it by numbers instead of names, so as to give you

practice. First, how many came to school this morning?"

"Ten of us," answered the little De House-Mouses.

"Very good," said the teacher. "Now, remember the lesson. How many are five and four?"

"Five and four are ten," answered the mouse children.

"Very good," said Miss Tabby. "And I am relieved to find that none of you have strayed away during the day. Now run home, all ten of you."

The next day the nine children came, and they were divided into classes of five and four, and the lesson was that five and three are nine, and Sleekness was put into the closet. Miss Tabby again called the roll by numbers, and again convinced Mrs. De House-Mouse that nine children left school at dismissal.

And Mrs. De House-Mouse said it was very annoying, but she never did have any head for the higher mathematics.

The third day the little De House-Mouses learned that four and three were eight, and Cuteness was put into the closet.

And the fourth day three and three were seven.

And the fifth day two and three were six.

And the sixth day two and two were five.

And the seventh day two and one were four.

And the eighth day one and one were three.

And meanwhile, Fatness, Spryness, Soft-Foot, Long-Tail and Bright-Eyes had all gone into the closet.

The ninth day only Whiskerando and White-Tooth were left to go to school. Miss Tabby taught them that one and none were two, and promptly put White-Tooth into the closet for disputing it.

When the time came for dismissal, Miss Tabby smiled so broadly that it seemed as if her head would fall off, and asked Whiskerando how many were in his class.

"One," answered Whiskerando, quickly.

"Very good. And how many are in the other class?"

"None," answered Whiskerando, timidly.

"Very well answered," said Miss Cat. "And you are a very bright scholar, Whiskerando. Now, how many are one and none?"

"T-two," stuttered poor Whiskerando.

"Excellent!" cried Miss Cat. "Now the two of you may run home!"

"B-but, t-teacher," stammered Whiskerando, "there aren't two of us to go home! There's only me, and that's one!"

"Dear, dear!" said Miss Cat, licking her lips. "You simply have not learned your lesson, have you? The doors are all locked and the windows are all closed, and yet you dare to dispute me. Now again, how many are one and none?"

"Two," said Whiskerando, weakly.

"Well, then, if I should eat one of you, there would still be one remaining. And if, as you say, you are the only one, then the remaining one will be you, will it not?"

Then Whiskerando saw what Miss Cat had been plotting all along, and knew that he would have to use his wits if he wanted to escape.

"Yes'm. But if you should eat me, by mistake, instead of the other one, then how could the other one go to tell my mother that you sent home two of us?"

"Ah, hum!" said the teacher. "Well, run along home, and tell your mother I sent

MISS TABITHA CAT—
HOUSE KINDERGARTEN
NUMBERS A SPECIALTY

home two of you, and be sure you come back
bright and early tomorrow."

She opened the door and Whiskerando
slipped past her, and tipping his head on one
side, said, "Yes'm. And tomorrow you will

teach me that none and none are one, won't you, ma'am?" And he whisked away.

"Dear me!" said Miss Cat. "I do believe that that little mouse was making fun of me. I am sure he intends never to come back. Well," she purred, putting out her long, pink tongue and smiling, "I still have his nine brothers and sisters in the closet, and as I am very hungry, I think I'll begin on them right now."

She went to the closet, opened the door a crack, and called, "White-Tooth, Fatness, Bright-Eyes, Spryness, Long-Tail, Cuteness, Soft-Foot, Sleekness, Blackieback!"

She opened the door very cautiously a little more, and a little more, and then threw it wide open, but all she saw was a hole in one corner and a note at the edge of it addressed to herself in mouse-track writing.

In great haste she opened the note and read:

Dear Teacher of Numbers,
Nine from nine leaves how many?
Your loving pupils.

This made Miss Tabitha Cat so angry that she promptly went out of the house and took in her sign.

THE PATIENT CAT

By *LAURA E. RICHARDS*

WHEN the spotted cat first found the nest, there was nothing in it. It was only just finished. So she said, "I will wait!" for she was a patient cat, and the whole summer was before her.

She waited a week, and then she climbed up again to the top of the tree and peeked into the nest. There lay two lovely blue eggs, smooth and shining. But the spotted cat said, "Eggs may be good, but young birds are better. I will wait!"

So she waited—and while she was waiting, she caught mice and rats, and washed herself, and slept, and did all that a spotted cat should do to pass the time away.

Then, when another week had passed, she climbed the tree again and peeked into the nest. This time there were five eggs. But the spotted cat said again, "Eggs may be good, but young birds are better. I will wait a little longer!" So she waited a little longer, and then went up again to look. Ah! There were five little, tiny birds, with big eyes and long necks, and yellow beaks wide open.

14

Then the spotted cat sat down on the branch and licked her nose, and purred, for she was very happy. "It is worth while to be patient!" she said.

But when she looked again at the young birds, to see which one she should take first, she saw that they were very thin. Oh, so very, *very*, VERY thin they were!

"Now," she said to herself, "if I were to wait only a few days longer, they would grow very fat. Thin birds may be good, but fat birds are much better. I will wait!"

So she waited—and she watched the big birds bringing worms all day long to the nest. "Aha!" she said. "They must be fattening very fast!"

At last, one day she thought, "Surely, now they must be fat enough. I will not wait another day. Ah, how good they will be!"

So she climbed up the tree, licking her lips all the way, and thinking of the fat young birds. But when she reached the top and looked into the nest, it was empty!

Then the spotted cat sat down on the branch and said, "Well, of all the mean, *ungrateful* creatures I *ever* saw, those birds are the meanest! Meow!"

TOPSY'S BABIES

By *JANE L. HOXIE*

"I MUST teach the kittens some tricks," said Alice one day. "They are getting big. Don't you think they are old enough to learn to do things, Mother?"

"Well, suppose you try teaching them," said Mother.

So Alice went to the door and called, "Kittens! Kittens! Kittens! Come, Tip! Come, Trot! Come, kittens! (Now, their real names were Tipkins and Trotkins, but Alice always called them Tip and Trot for short.)

When the kittens heard the little girl call, they came running as fast as their fluffy little bodies and their short little legs would let them come—for "Kittens! Kittens! Kittens!" almost always meant, "Here's some nice warm milk to drink."

Alice gathered the funny little things up in her arms. They looked just exactly alike, for Tipkins had a black spot on the end of his tail, and Trotkins had a black spot on the end of his tail, too. Tipkins' eyes were blue, and so were Trotkins'. Tipkins' nose was black and Trotkins' nose was black, too. Alice often wondered how their mother, Topsy, ever told them apart.

"Now," said the little girl, "you have grown to be such big kittens that it is time you learned to earn your dinner. What do you say to that?"

"Meow! Meow!" said Tipkins. "Meow! Meow!" said Trotkins. "Meow! Meow!" said Tipkins and Trotkins together . . . which seemed to mean, "We will do that—just show us how."

Alice took a tiny bit of meat in her fingers and let one of the kittens smell it. Then she said very slowly, "Now, roll over." The kitten liked the smell of the meat very much, so he said, "Meow! Meow!" but he did not know in the least what "roll over" meant, so he did nothing. "Roll over, kitty," said the little girl again, but he only said, "Meow! Meow! Meow!" once more. Then Alice made the kitten lie down, and she gently rolled him over with her hand, saying very slowly as she did so, "Roll over!" After this, she gave him a piece of the meat.

Then it was the other kitten's turn. He had no more idea than his brother what "roll over" meant, but after Alice had said the words two or three times, she gently rolled his plump little body over, too, and then gave him a bit of meat also. Then she set a big saucer of milk down in front of her pets, and so ended the first lesson of Tipkins and Trotkins.

This was only the first of many lessons, however. Alice worked patiently with the kittens every day for a whole month and, at the end of that time, both Tipkins and Trotkins knew just what she meant and would roll over every time she told them to.

Tipkins seemed to think it was great fun,

and he would sometimes roll over five or six times without stopping, just as Alice herself often rolled on the grass when at play. But Trotkins never seemed to like doing it, and would turn round and round until he was fairly dizzy before finally lying down. Then, as he rolled over, he would give a funny meow, as much as to say, "I don't like to, but if I must, I will."

Tipkins learned to ring a small bell by striking it with one of his front paws. Trotkins could never be coaxed to touch this

bell, but he would sit by while his brother rang it and cry, "Meow! Meow! Meow!" Alice thought that this was very funny, and she said that Trot sang while Tip did the playing.

Both of the kittens learned to jump over a stick when their mistress held one out in her hand about a foot from the floor. And Alice taught Tipkins to jump through a small wooden hoop. But she could never persuade Trotkins even once to try to jump through the hoop.

As Tipkins and Trotkins grew older, their mother, Topsy, taught them to hunt for mice in the big barn, and to catch grasshoppers in the field. They had less and less time, as the days went by, to play with Alice. And Alice found them so sleepy when they did have time, that at last she gave up trying to teach them any new tricks.

As the months passed by, they grew sleek and fat. They were kittens no longer, but had grown as large and could hunt as well as Mother Topsy. And although they learned no new tricks now, the old ones, taught to them by Alice, were never forgotten by Tipkins and Trotkins.

PUSSY PUFF AND SNOWBALL

By ELIZABETH LINCOLN GOULD

Pussy Puff and Snowball,
Best of kitten friends,
Drinking milk together,
Eating odds and ends;
Both so clean and happy,
Little claws all sheathed,
A better pair of kittens
Surely never breathed.

"Pussy Puff," said Snowball,
"We must learn to write.
Here are pen and paper—
Let's begin tonight.
Who'll try first?" "Oh, Snowball,"
Pussy Puff said, "You,
For I am very sleepy.
Won't tomorrow do?"

Snowball's feeling sulky,
Cross as cross can be.
They were playing "Catch me!"
Pussy Puff and she,
When her mistress caught her,
Said, "Oh, Snowball, dear,
I must take your picture—
Now sit still right here."

Pussy Puff's in mischief!
See the spools of thread,
And the darning cotton,
And the cushion red,
With the silver thimble
And the box of pins.
When they're all tipped over,
Then the fun begins.

Pussy Puff and Snowball
Both begin to feel
It is time for supper
Or some other meal.
They can smell the cooking,
They can see the food,
So they wait together,
Very still and good.

TABBY FINDS A HOME

By LYDIA A. STRYKER

TABBY was worried. Anyone who knew anything at all about cats would have known that by the way she tried to bring all of her five kittens closer and closer to her warm body, and by the anxious tone of her voice when she spoke to them. (For a mother cat *does* talk to her babies, and the funny, furry little ones understand her, even if people do not.)

The north wind blew cold that night. It swept in under the barn, even to the farthest corner, where Tabby lived. The kittens shivered and mewed faint little cries. Their mother cuddled them all as close to her as she could, but she could not keep them very warm.

"It is very unkind for people to move and leave their cats behind," thought Tabby.

It seemed to grow colder every minute. When morning came, she slipped away, very softly, while the kittens were asleep. She wanted to find a new home. First she tried the big barn. The hayloft would make a soft, warm house.

"Bow-wow! Go away!" said the dog. Tabby had to climb a fence to get away from him.

How she did search! Into every box, under porches, under sheds, high and low, but not a place could she find. She was trotting along over the fences when she saw Miss Emily. Why Tabby thought that Miss Emily would help her, no one knows. But she stopped and looked at Miss Emily, and meowed. It was such an anxious, worried meow that Miss Emily looked up at once. She liked cats.

"Poor pussy, what is the matter?"

"Meow!" said Tabby.

"Are you hungry? Come in the house. I'll give you something."

Tabby was very glad to get the milk. She had not had any breakfast. After she had lapped it up, she rubbed against Miss Emily to say thank you. Then she went to the door. "Meow!" she said.

Miss Emily opened the door, and Tabby went out and hurried back to her kittens. She had decided to take them all to Miss Emily. She was sure Miss Emily would help. She would understand how much the kittens needed a home where it was warm.

Tabby picked up one of the kittens very carefully by the loose skin on the back of the neck and started off.

It was a strange way to carry her babies, in her mouth, but it was the best way she could do it.

When she reached Miss Emily's, the door was shut again.

"Meow!" said Tabby.

Miss Emily opened the door, and Tabby walked in and placed the kitten at Miss Emily's feet. "Meow!" she said.

"Dear me!" said Miss Emily. "I think I don't want a kitten."

"Meow! Meow! Oh, please!" said Tabby.
"How many more are there?"

"Meow!" said Tabby, going to the door.

"Well, go and get them," said Miss Emily, laughing. "I'll see what I can do." And Tabby ran through the door.

Four times after that, Tabby went back and forth, carrying her babies. She was tired but happy when she placed the last one at Miss Emily's feet.

"What do you want me to do with them?" asked Miss Emily. Tabby rubbed against her and purred. She was sure that whatever Miss Emily did would be right.

Miss Emily brought a box from the cellar. She folded a piece of carpet and placed it in the bottom of the box. She put the box in a warm place by the stove. Then she took the kittens and put them, one by one, into the box. Tabby watched her. When they were all in, she jumped in, too. She looked up at Miss Emily and purred her thanks. No matter how cold it was, she would not have to worry now. There would always be plenty to eat and a warm place to sleep in her new home. As she snuggled down, she purred happily.

COPY CAT

By *MOLLY C. RODMAN*

COPY CAT was a silly little kitten.
  She always watched to see what every-body else did.
  She never made up any games for herself.
  She never even tried to think of a new way to catch mice,
  Or chase butterflies.
  Copy Cat was lazy.

She wanted everybody else in the world to think.

Then she would borrow their ideas.

But no one could borrow any ideas from Copy Cat,

Because she didn't have even *one* idea that was all her own!

Of course, even so, she was a very unusual little kitten.

She could meow like her father,

Or her mother—

Or any other cat's meow.

But she didn't have a meow that was all her own!

She could even bark like a puppy

And quack like a duck.

She could wriggle her nose like a rabbit,

And growl like a bear.

She could chatter like a squirrel

And run like a deer.

Copy Cat could be almost everybody else,

But she couldn't be *herself!*

She had never even *tried* to be!

Whenever any of the other animals saw Copy Cat coming,

They ran away.

Nobody wanted to be her friend.

Not even the snails she tried to play with.

The snails didn't like her because she pretended

To have a house on her back just like theirs.

And horns on her head just like theirs!

And she even tried to slide across the ground the very same way they did.

So whenever they saw Copy Cat coming, the snails crawled into their houses

And locked the doors.

They would not come out again until she went away.

One day Copy Cat saw a little mouse.

She did not try to catch it.

But she sat and watched to see what it would do,

So that she could do the very same thing!

The mouse ran through the hole in the garden fence.

"I can do the same thing!" said Copy Cat.

So she stuck her head through the hole in the garden fence.

But the rest of her wasn't little enough to follow her head.

And there she was—stuck in the mouse's fence hole,

With her head in his front door

And her feet and tail in his front yard!

She did not know what to do

Because there was nobody to watch

To see what they would do!

When Copy Cat found that she didn't know how to do anything else,

She started to meow.

But it was not her *own* meow, because—

She had never had a meow of her own!

First, she meowed like her father.

She meowed like all the other cats,

But nobody came to rescue her.

For how could any of the other animals know it was Copy Cat,

When she had everybody else's voice, but no meow of her own?

She even tried to quack like a duck,
But nothing happened.

She tried to bark like a puppy,
But nothing happened.

She tried to wiggle her nose like a rabbit,
And growl like a bear.

She didn't feel at all like chattering like a squirrel.

And as much as she wanted to, she couldn't run like a deer now!

It isn't often that any mouse feels sorry for a cat.

But this mouse wasn't a "Copy Mouse,"
And so he didn't think exactly the same kind of thoughts that most mice did.

He stood right in front of Copy Cat's mouth, even though

She might have opened it up and swallowed him right down.

But right now, Copy Cat didn't feel like eating anybody!

The garden fence, however, was not as strong as it felt.

The mouse looked at Copy Cat and thought very hard.

"It will take an explosion of some kind to get you out of here!" he said finally.

Then he picked up a piece of straw and started tickling Copy Cat's whiskers with it.

"KER-CHOO! KER-CHOO!"

Copy Cat sneezed so hard that some of the boards in the fence came tumbling down.

The mouse tickled her whiskers with the straw again.

"KER-CHOO!" Copy Cat sneezed harder than ever.

And this time the mouse's front door looked almost big enough for an elephant's front door!

Now Copy Cat was free. But what about the mouse?

Suddenly, she caught him in her paws the way she had seen other cats do.

If she couldn't do everything a mouse did, then she would eat him for dinner just the same way other cats did.

"Why should you eat me after I saved your life?" the mouse asked. "Do you think most of the other mice would bother about trying to save a cat's life? Why, if I had been a Copy Mouse, I would have let you stay there!"

It was true. The mouse had tried to be her friend. He had saved her life. He was a very nice mouse.

Suddenly, the kitten opened up her paws and purred at him. And it wasn't anybody else's purr. It was her very own purr, one that she had thought up all by herself.

The mouse looked into her big green eyes.

He squeaked happily:

"Most mice don't like cats, and most cats eat mice. "But *we* don't have to be 'Copy cats,' do we?"

THE POPOCATEPETLS

By SOPHIA T. NEWMAN

"TWO KITTENS! I thought Mrs. Bruce was going to let you choose only one," said Mother Dale.

"Yes, Mom," said Phillip, "but we didn't know which kitten to choose, so Mrs. Bruce put them all on the floor. We called to the kittens to see which one would come, and every time we called, these two came running toward us."

"Always the same two, Mom," chimed in Bessie, "and can't we keep them? Please!"

Who could resist such eager little faces? Not Mother Dale. "They are very pretty little malties," she said, smiling. "How can you tell them apart?"

The children lifted the kittens' heads, showing a white spot in the fur on each little neck.

"Bibs!" cried big sister Edith. "And Bessie's kitten has the larger one! What will you call them?"

"I'm going to call mine Popocatepetl," said Phillip, who was learning about Mexico in school.

"What?" laughed Mother and Edith together.

"I want to call mine Poppytoppykettle, too!" cried Bessie.

"You might name them both Popocatepetl," said Edith, still laughing, "and call one by the first end, Popo, and the other by the last, Petl."

"And Pop and Pet for short," added Mother.

Once adopted, Pop and Pet became favored members of the household. They developed all the playful and amusing ways common to kittens, and according to the Dale family, a great many uncommon ones, also. Even Father Dale, on whose knees the kittens sat while he read his evening paper, declared that they never made a mistake, Pop always taking the right knee and Pet the left. They certainly were wonderful kittens!

It was when the Popocatepetls had grown to be of good size that Phillip and Bessie came in one day with a jet-black kitten, very glossy, very small, and very pretty.

"Children!"

"He was all lost, Mom!" cried Bess, breathless with excitement.

"And he followed us all the way from school," added Phillip.

"Is he going to be a Popocatepetl, too?" asked Edith, mischievously. "You can call him by the middle of the name, you know, and make it Cat."

"May we, Mom?"

Mother was doubtful, but when Father came home, he was positive.

"This is too much, children," he said. "You cannot have three cats. You must give one of them away."

"Oh, Dad, we can't spare Pop or Pet, and

Cat is so cute! Oh, look at him now, swinging on the chair!"

"Isn't he just the cutest—"

"Do you hear what I say?" interrupted Father Dale. "You may keep whichever two you choose, but the third one you must give away in the morning."

Phillip and Bessie retreated to the broad window-seat in the hall. Their mournful little voices now and then reached the room where the older ones sat reading, although all seemed uncomfortable because the little ones were unhappy.

Suddenly Edith put down her book and left the room. A few minutes later, a peal of childish laughter rang out.

"What a way Edith has with the children!" said Mr. Dale, looking relieved as the laughter rang out again.

"She is a dear girl," said Mrs. Dale. "I wonder what they are laughing at."

Now it so happened that the next day was Mr. Dale's birthday, and when he came down in the morning, he found upon his chair a covered basket. To its handle was tied a card:

For Dad. With love from Phillip and Bessie. Many happy returns!

"Mew!" came faintly from within the basket. Then the cover stirred, and up peeked Cat's little black face!

Mr. Dale placed Cat on his shoulder, and laughed till the tears came.

"Come here, you little rascals!" he called to the children, peeking in at the door. "A man can't refuse his own birthday present!"

So the three Popocatepetls stayed with the Dales, and were "happy ever after."

DICK WHITTINGTON AND HIS CAT

IN THE reign of the famous King Edward III, there was a little boy called Dick Whittington, whose father and mother died when he was very young. Since poor Dick was not old enough to work, he was very badly off. He got but little for his dinner, and sometimes nothing at all for his breakfast; for the people who lived in the village were very poor indeed, and could not spare him much more than the parings of potatoes, and now and then a hard crust of bread.

Now Dick had heard many, many very strange things about the great city called London. The country people at that time thought that folks in London were all fine gentlemen and ladies . . . and that there was singing and music there all day long . . . and that the streets were all paved with gold.

One day a large wagon and eight horses, all with bells at their heads, drove through the village while Dick was standing by the sign-post. He thought this wagon must be going to London, so he asked the driver to let him walk with him by the side of the wagon. When the driver heard that poor Dick had no father or mother, and saw by his ragged clothes that he could not be worse off than he was, he told him he might go if he would, so off they set together.

Dick got to London, and was in such a hurry to see the fine streets paved all over with gold, that he did not even stay to thank the kind driver. He ran off as fast as his legs would carry him, through many of the streets, thinking every moment to come to those that were paved with gold. Dick had seen a guinea three times in his own little village, and re-membered what a great deal of money it brought in change; so he thought he had nothing to do but to take up some little bits of the pavement, and he would then have as much money as he could wish for.

Poor Dick ran till he was tired, and had quite forgotten his friend the driver. But at last, when it grew dark, and he found that every way he turned there was nothing but dirt instead of gold, he sat down in a dark corner and cried himself to sleep.

Little Dick was all night in the streets. Next morning, being very hungry, he got up and walked about. He asked everybody he met to give him a halfpenny to keep him from starving, but nobody stayed to answer him, and only two or three gave him a halfpenny, so that the poor boy was quite weak and faint for the want of food.

In his distress he begged several people for money and one of them said crossly: "Go to work, you idle rogue!"

"That I will," said Dick, "I will go to work for you, if you will let me." But the man only muttered and went on.

At last a good-natured looking gentleman saw how hungry he looked. "Why don't you go to work, my lad?" he said to Dick.

"That I would, but I do not know how to get any," answered Dick.

"If you are willing, come along with me," said the gentleman, and took him to a hayfield, where Dick worked briskly and lived merrily till the hay was made.

After this, he found himself as badly off as before. And being almost starved again, he went to the door of Mr. Fitzwarren, a rich merchant. Here he was soon seen by the cook, who was quite ill-tempered, and happened just then to be very busy preparing dinner. She called out to poor Dick: "What business do you have here, you lazy rogue? There is nothing else but beggars. If you do not take yourself away, we will see how you will like a dousing of dishwater. I have some here hot enough to make you jump."

Just at that time Mr. Fitzwarren himself came home to dinner. When he saw a ragged boy lying at the door, he said to him: "Why do you lie there, my boy? You seem old enough to work. I am afraid you are inclined to be lazy."

"No, indeed, sir," said Dick to him. "That is not the case, for I would work with all my heart, but I do not know anybody, and I believe I am very sick for the want of food."

"Poor fellow! Get up—let me see what ails you."

Dick now tried to rise, but had to lie down again, being too weak to stand, for he had not eaten any food for three days, and was no longer able to run about and beg a halfpenny of people in the streets. So the kind merchant ordered him to be taken into the house, and have a good dinner given him, and be kept to do what work he was able to do for the cook.

Little Dick would have lived very happily in this good family if it had not been for the ill-natured cook. She used to say: "You are under me, so look sharp. Clean the spit and the dripping-pan, make the fires, wind up the jack, and do all the scullery work nimbly, or —" and she would shake the ladle at him. Besides, she was so fond of basting, that when she had no meat to baste, she would baste poor Dick's head and shoulders with a broom, or anything else that happened to fall in her way.

At last her ill-usage of him was told to Alice, Mr. Fitzwarren's daughter, who told the cook she would be dismissed if she did not treat him more kindly.

The behavior of the cook was now a little better. But besides this, Dick had another hardship to get over. His bed stood in a garret, where there were so many holes in the floor and the walls that every night he was annoyed with rats and mice. A gentleman

having given Dick a penny for cleaning his
shoes, he thought he would buy a cat with it.
The next day he saw a girl with a cat, and
asked her, "Will you let me have that cat for
a penny?" The girl said: "Yes, I will, though
she is an excellent mouser."

Dick hid his cat in the garret, and always
remembered to bring back with him a part

of his dinner for her. In a short time he had no more trouble with rats and mice, but slept soundly every night.

Soon after this, his master had a ship ready to sail. As it was the custom that all his servants have some chance for good fortune as well as himself, he called them all into the parlor and asked them what they would like to send out for trade.

They all had something that they were willing to trade except poor Dick, who had neither money nor goods, and therefore could send nothing. For this reason he did not come into the parlor with the rest. But Miss Alice guessed what was the matter, and ordered him to be called in. She then said: "I will lay down some money for him, from my own purse." But her father told her: "This will not do, for it must be something of his own."

When poor Dick heard this, he said: "I have nothing but a cat which I bought for a penny some time ago from a little girl."

"Fetch your cat, then, my lad," said Mr. Fitzwarren, "and let her go."

Dick went upstairs and brought down poor puss, with tears in his eyes, and gave her to the captain. "For," he said, "I shall now be

kept awake all night by the rats and mice."
Everyone laughed at Dick's odd venture—
and Miss Alice, who felt sorry for him, gave
him some money to buy another cat.

This, and many other marks of kindness
shown him by Miss Alice, made the ill-tempered cook jealous of poor Dick, and she began to use him more cruelly than ever, and always made fun of him for sending his cat to
sea. She asked him: "Do you think your cat
will sell for as much money as would buy a
stick to beat you?"

At last poor Dick could bear it no longer,
and he decided to run away. He packed up
his few things, and started very early in the
morning, on All Saints' Day, the first of November. He walked as far as Halloway—and
there sat down on a stone, which to this day
is called "Whittington's Stone," and began to
consider which road to take.

While he was thinking what he should do,
the Bells of Bow Church, which at the time
were only six, began to ring, and at their
sound seemed to say to him:

"Turn again, Whittington,
Thrice Lord Mayor of London."

"Lord Mayor of London!" said he to himself. "Why, to be sure, I would put up with almost anything now, to be Lord Mayor of London and ride a fine coach when I grow to be a man! I will go back, and think nothing of the cuffing and scolding of the old cook, if I am to be Lord Mayor of London at last."

Dick went back, and was lucky to get into the house and set about his work before the old cook came downstairs.

We must now follow Miss Puss to the coast of Africa. The ship with the cat on board was a long time at sea, and was at last driven by the winds on a part of the coast of Barbary, where the only people were the Moors, unknown to the English. The people came in great numbers to see the sailors, and treated them well, and, when they became better acquainted, were very eager to buy the fine things that the ship contained.

When the captain saw this, he sent patterns of the best things he had to the king of the country, who was so much pleased with them, that he asked the captain to come to the palace. Here they were placed, as is the custom of the country, on rich carpets flowered with gold and silver. The king and queen were seated at the upper end of the room, and a number of dishes were brought in for dinner. They had not sat long, when a great number of rats and mice rushed in, and ate all the meat in an instant. The captain wondered at this, and asked if these vermin were not unpleasant.

"Oh, yes," they said. "They are very offensive, and the king would give half his treasure to be freed of them, for they not only eat his dinner, as you see, but they attack him in his chamber, and even in bed, so that he is obliged to be watched while he is sleeping, for fear of them."

The captain jumped for joy. He remembered poor Whittington and his cat, and told the king he had an animal on board the ship that would take care of all these vermin immediately.

The king was so delighted at this news that his turban dropped off his head. "Bring this creature to me," he said. "Vermin are dreadful in a court, and if she will do what you say, I will load your ship with gold and jewels in exchange for her."

The captain, who knew his business, took this opportunity to set forth the merits of Miss Puss. He told his majesty: "It is not very convenient to part with her, as, when she is gone, the rats and mice may destroy the goods in the ship—but to oblige your majesty, I will fetch her."

"Run, run!" said the queen. "I am impatient to see the dear creature."

Away went the captain to the ship, while another dinner was prepared. He put Puss under his arm, and arrived at the place just in time to see the table full of rats. When the cat saw them, she did not wait for bidding, but jumped out of the captain's arms, and in a few minutes laid almost all the rats and mice dead

at her feet. The rest of them in their fright
scampered away to their holes.

The king was quite charmed to get rid of
such plagues so easily, and the queen desired
that the creature who had done them so great
a kindness might be brought to her, that she
might look at her. Upon which the captain
called: "Pussy, pussy, pussy!" and she came
to him.

He then presented her to the queen, who

started back, and was afraid to touch a creature who had made such a havoc among the rats and mice. However, when the captain stroked the cat and called: "Pussy, pussy," the queen also touched her and cried: "Putty, putty," for she had not learned English. He then put her down on the queen's lap, where she purred and played with her majesty's hand, and then purred herself to sleep.

The king, having seen what Miss Puss could do, and being informed that her kittens would stock the whole country, and keep it free from rats, bargained with the captain for the whole ship's cargo, and then gave him ten times as much for the cat as all the rest amounted to.

The captain then took leave of the royal party, and set sail with a fair wind for England, and after a happy voyage arrived safe in London.

One morning, early, Mr. Fitzwarren had just come to his countinghouse and seated himself at the desk to count over the cash and settle the business for the day, when somebody rapped at the door.

"Who's there?" said Mr. Fitzwarren.

"A friend," answered the other. "I come to bring you good news of your ship *Unicorn*."

The merchant, bustling up in such a hurry that he forgot his gout, opened the door, and who should he see waiting but the captain with a cabinet of jewels and a bill of lading. When he looked at this, the merchant lifted up his eyes and thanked Heaven for bringing about such a prosperous voyage.

They then told the story of the cat, and showed the rich present that the king and queen had sent for her to poor Dick. As soon as the merchant heard this, he called out to his servants:

"Go send him in, and tell him of his fame—
And call him Mr. Whittington by name."

Mr. Fitzwarren now showed himself to be a good man; for when some of his servants said so great a treasure was too much for him, he answered: "God forbid I should deprive him of the value of a single penny. It is his own, and he shall have it all."

He then sent for Dick, who at that time was scouring pots for the cook, and was quite dirty. He would have excused himself from coming into the countinghouse, saying, "That room is swept, and my shoes are dirty and

full of hobnails." But the merchant ordered
him to come in.

Mr. Fitzwarren ordered a chair to be set
for him, and so he began to think they were
making fun of him, and at the same time said
to them: "Do not play tricks with a poor sim-
ple boy, but let me go down again, if you
please, to my work."

"Indeed, Mr. Whittington," said the merchant, "we are all quite in earnest with you,

and I most heartily rejoice in the news that these gentlemen have brought you; for the captain has sold your cat to the King of Barbary, and brought you in return for her more riches than I possess in the whole world. I wish that you may long enjoy them!"

Mr. Fitzwarren then told the men to open the great treasure they had brought with them, and said: "Mr. Whittington has nothing to do but to put it in some place of safety."

Poor Dick hardly knew how to behave himself for joy. He begged his master to take what part of it he pleased, since he owed it all to his kindness. "No, no," answered Mr. Fitzwarren, "this is all your own—and I have no doubt but you will use it well."

Dick next asked his mistress, and then Miss Alice, to accept a part of his good fortune; but they would not, and at the same time told him they felt great joy at his good success. But this poor fellow was too kind-hearted to keep it all to himself, so he made a present to the captain, the mate, and the rest of Mr. Fitzwarren's servants—and even to the ill-natured old cook.

After this, Mr. Fitzwarren advised him to send for a proper tailor, and get himself dressed like a gentleman; and told him he was welcome to live in his house till he could provide himself a better one.

When Whittington's face was washed, his hair curled, his hat cocked, and he was dressed in a nice suit of clothes, he was as handsome as any young man who visited at Mr. Fitzwarren's; so that Miss Alice, who had once been so kind to him, and thought of him with pity, now looked upon him as fit to be her sweetheart; and the more so, no doubt, because Whittington was now always thinking what he could do to oblige her, and making her the prettiest presents that could be.

Mr. Fitzwarren soon saw their love for each other and proposed to join them in marriage. To this they both readily agreed. A day for the wedding was soon fixed.

History tells us that Mr. Whittington and his lady lived in great splendor, and were very happy. They had several children. He was Sheriff of London, thrice Lord Mayor, and received the honor of knighthood by Henry V.

The figure of Sir Richard Whittington with his cat in his arms, carved in stone, was to be seen till the year 1780 over the archway of a prison at Newgate.

THE LITTLE GRAY KITTEN

By MARY LAURENCE TURNBULL

ONCE there was a little gray kitten who wandered far away from home. At first she liked all the strange sights she saw, but by and by she began to feel very homesick, and wished she was once more cuddled up to her brothers and sisters.

The only word that this little gray kitten knew was "Mew!" So, when she was lonely, she would say, "Mew!" When she was hungry, it was "Mew!" too. When she was cold or tired, glad or sad, it was always "Mew!" At home they knew what she meant when she said, "Mew!" But out in the wide, wide world, nobody seemed to know.

Wandering along the street, she came upon a little squirming earthworm. "Mew!" she said, meaning, "Where is my home?"

The earthworm, however, did not notice the little gray kitten, but crawled away across the street.

Next, the little gray kitten met a butterfly that was resting on top of a dandelion.

"Mew!" said the little gray kitten, meaning, "Can you tell me where my home is?"

But the butterfly did not say anything, and flew away.

The little gray kitten walked on, and then she saw a robin on a stone wall nearby. "Mew!" said the little gray kitten. "Where is my home?"

But the robin, cocking his head on one side, answered, "Chirp, chirp," and then, spreading his wings, flew away.

She felt very sad, indeed, but running along, she came up to a big black dog. "Mew, mew!" said the little gray kitten. "Can't you tell me where my home is?"

But the big black dog shook his head and barked, "Bow-wow, bow-wow, bow-wow!" so loudly that the little gray kitten ran away from him as fast as she could go.

The little gray kitten was very tired, but she still ran on, and soon met a big red cow. "Mew, mew!" said the little gray kitten. "Can't you tell me where my home is?"

The big red cow, however, hardly looking at the little kitten, stretched out her big head and said, "Moo, moo-o-o!" which so frightened the little gray kitten that she jumped over a fence and landed right in the middle of a flower bed.

There she caught sight of a little girl running up to her, and with such a sweet smile on her face that the little gray kitten ran toward her and said once more, "Mew! Do you know where my home is?"

"Oh, you dear, fluffy gray ball!" said the smiling little girl, catching the kitten up in her arms. "I'm going to take you right home to live with me."

The little girl was the only one who had understood, and the little gray kitten purred softly. She was happy, for she had found a home at last.

WHY CATS ALWAYS LAND ON THEIR FEET

ONCE very long ago, a mighty magician traveling through a forest paused to rest and lie down at the foot of a tree. To the singing of birds, the buzzing of many insects, and the rustling of leaves stirred by a gentle wind, he closed his eyes and was soon fast asleep.

As he slumbered on the soft, green moss, a large, ugly serpent came from the thicket, making its way slowly toward the magician. Closer and closer it came, until it was almost upon him.

The magician moved restlessly in his sleep, and the serpent drew back for a moment. But then it saw the magician's eyes were shut, so once more it advanced.

"I will kill this man!" the serpent hissed as it recognized him. "He does not deserve to live, for it was he, last night, who kept me from having my supper. That cat would have made a fine meal, but I could not have it, and only because this man had warned it of my coming and caused it to run away." So saying, it made ready to strike.

But the serpent did not know that in the branches of the tree above the sleeping magician the little cat was hidden. It had seen the serpent slithering from the thicket.

Without hesitation, though its heart was full of fear, the cat leaped down upon the serpent, using its sharp claws to the fullest. The serpent struck wildly at the brave little cat, its eyes flashing fire, but the cat was too quick. It slashed at the serpent's head, until at last the creature lay dead.

Awakened by the commotion, the magician watched the battle, and when it was over, he said, "Little cat, you have saved my life, for which I thank you. But how can I reward you? Your eyes and ears are already quick to see and hear, and you can run very swiftly."

The magician thought for a long time. At last he said, "Ah! I believe I *can* do something for you. This shall be your gift. From this day forward, you shall be known as a friend of man, and you may call his home yours as well. Further, for as long as you live, you may leap where you wish and you shall always fall upon your feet."

It has been so to this very day.

HOW CATS CAME TO PURR

By *JOHN BENNETT*

A BOY, having a pet cat which he wished to feed, said to her, "Come, Cat, drink this dish of cream—it will keep your fur as soft as silk and make you purr like a coffee-mill."

He had no sooner said this than the cat, with a great glare of her green eyes, bristled her tail and went over the back fence, head first—*pop!* as mad as a wet hen.

And this is how she came to do so:

The story is an old one—very, very old. It may be Persian, it may be not—that is of very little importance. It is so old that if all the nine lives of all the cats that ever lived in the world were set up together in a line, the other end of it would just reach back to when this story took place.

And this is the story:

Many, many years ago, in a country which was very far away, there was a huge cat that ground the coffee in the King's kitchen, and helped with the meals.

This cat was, in truth, the first and very father of all cats, and his name was Sooty Will, for his fur was as black as a night in a coal mine. He was ninety years old, and his whiskers were like whisk brooms. But the most unusual thing about him was that in all his life, he had never once purred nor arched his back, although his master often stroked him. The fact was that he never had any reason, so far as he knew, for arching his back. And being the father of all cats, there was no one to tell him how. It remained for him to find a reason, and to set an example which cats have followed from that time forth, and will forever follow.

The King of the country had long been at war with one of his neighbors, but one morning he sent a messenger to say that he had beaten his enemy at last, and that he was coming home for an early breakfast as hungry as three bears. "Have wheat cakes and coffee ready," he declared. "Hot, and plenty of 'em!"

At that the turnspits danced and yelped with glee, for wheat cakes and coffee are not cooked upon spits, and so they were free to go forth into the city street and watch the King's homecoming in a grand parade.

They danced out into the courtyard, turning handsprings, headsprings and heelsprings as they went, and after giving three hearty cheers in a grand chorus at the bottom of the garden, went happily away for their holiday.

The cat hissed at their vanishing heels, sat down on his tail in the chimney corner, and was very glum, indeed.

Just then the cook looked in from the pantry. "Hello!" he said gruffly. "Come hurry up the coffee!" That was the way he always gave his orders.

The black cat's whiskers bristled. He

turned to the mill with a fierce frown, his
long tail going to and fro like that of a tiger
in its lair, for Sooty Will had a temper like
hot gunpowder that was apt to go off *sizz,*
whizz, bang! Yet, at least while the cook was
near, he turned and turned the mill as
though he didn't mind at all.

Meanwhile, out in the city, it was a glorious day. The sun shone brightly in the blue
sky, banners waved from the castle towers,
and the city gates rang with the cheers of
the happy crowd.

Then came the parade. First there were three regiments of trumpeters, all blowing different tunes, then fifteen regiments of mounted horsemen on coal-black horses, forty platoons of green and blue dragoons, and a thousand drummers and fifers in scarlet and blue and gold, and well up in the front of the ranks was the King himself, bowing and smiling to the people—a glorious sight, indeed!

Back in the kitchen, the black cat turned the coffee-mill. "My, oh, my!" he said. "It certainly is not fair that those bench-legged turnspits with feet like leather should see the King marching home in his glory, while I, who go, as they say, with feet of velvet, should only hear the sound through the pantry windows. It is not fair. A cat may look at a King. And if any cat may look at a King, why, I am the cat who may. There are no other cats in the world. I am the only one. The cook may shout till his breath gives out. He cannot frighten me. For once, I am going to have my fling."

And in an instant, he swallowed the coffee-mill—box, handle, knobs, and all—and was off to see the King.

When the parade was past and gone, and all the people were back in their homes, Sooty Will, with drooping tail, stood by the palace gate. He was very unhappy. Indeed, who would *not* be, with a coffee-mill in his stomach!

Suddenly the cook popped his head out the window and cried, "How, now, you lazybones! The parade is done, but the breakfast is not. Hurry! The cakes are all cooked and piping hot! Why is the coffee so slow?"

The King was in the dining hall, in dressing gown and slippers, calling for his breakfast!

The guilty cat quickly ran down the back stairs and hid under the refrigerator. He was so ashamed that he dared not look the kind cook in the face. He began to cry.

The cook came into the room and seeing the cat, he said, "Where is the coffee?"

"Someone must have come into the kitchen while I ran out to look at the King!" the cat gasped, for there seemed to him no way out but by telling a little lie. And with that, choking upon the handle of the mill, which was sticking in his throat, he burst into sobs.

70

The cook, who was a very kind-hearted man, tried to comfort the poor cat. "There, there, do not weep!" he said. "There are always thieves to be found in King's houses!" And, stooping, he stroked the drooping cat's back to show that he did not blame him.

Sooty Will's heart leaped into his throat.

"Oh, oh!" he half gasped. "Oh, oh! If he rubs his hand down my back, he will feel the corners of the coffee-mill through my ribs. Oh, oh! I am a gone cat!" And with that, for fear that he would be found out, he arched his back as high in the air as he could, so that the corners of the mill would not show at his sides.

71

But, alas! He forgot that coffee-mills turn. As he arched his back to hide his guilt, the coffee-mill inside rolled over—and as it rolled, it began to grind—*rr-rrr-rrr-rrr-rrr!*

"Oh, oh! You have swallowed the mill!" cried the cook.

"No, no," cried the cat, "I was only thinking aloud."

At that, out stepped a Wizard, and with his finger pointed at the cat, said in a terrible voice, "For what you have done, from this day forward, whenever men stroke you in kindness, you shall remember your guilt and arch your back with shame, as you did now in order not to be found out. And so, whenever man is kind to a cat, the sound of the grinding of a coffee-mill inside shall forever remind him of your guilt and shame."

With that, the Wizard vanished in a cloud of smoke.

From that day on, Sooty Will could never have his back stroked without arching it to hide the mill within him. And never did he arch his back but the coffeemill began to grind *rr-rrr-rrr!* inside him. And as the great Wizard said, so it has been for all cats, even to the present day.

THE MAILBAG KITTEN

By ESTELLE M. HART

KITTEN FLUFF was born in a round basket in the back room of the Rushtown Post Office. It was there, with her two sisters, Kitten Gray and Kitten Spot, that she spent the first days of her life.

For the first week or two the kittens were happy. All they wanted to do was to eat and sleep, and Mother Muff attended to their meals and kept the house (the basket, that is) very quiet while they slept.

One day they found out two things: one, that the world wasn't just their basket; the other, that their legs were made to walk with. It was a great deal of trouble to make their legs go the way they wanted at first, but after a few days' practice they found that their legs would not only go where they wanted to have them go, but would go very fast, too.

What fun they had when they found that out! How they scampered after each other —and after Mother Muff, if she happened to go to the door to see what the weather was like!

Mother Muff was very proud of her kittens. She said to herself that they were the smartest family of kittens she had ever had —and, as they were the *only* ones she had ever had, she was quite right!

One day they went through the door into the post office. What a large place it was! Kitten Gray and Kitten Fluff examined all the desks and chairs, every nook and corner, and got acquainted with Postmaster Jones and the clerks. But it was Kitten Spot who found the mailbags. There they were—flat, empty things, thrown in a pile in a corner.

74

"What a fine place to lie down and take a nap!" thought Kitten Spot, curling herself into a little ball on the leather bags.

Kitten Gray and Kitten Fluff thought that they were very tired, too. Following Kitten Spot's example, they cuddled down beside her and were fast asleep in a minute.

When Mother Muff walked in, a short time later, she was shocked to discover where her children were sleeping. She knew that mailbags were very important. She had heard that people who tampered with mailbags were punished. She was almost sure she heard a step outside.

She picked up the kittens one at a time by the back of their necks, and hurried along to their good, safe basket. Then she gave them a scolding she was sure they would never forget.

But whenever they went into the post office, the kittens always felt so sleepy when they got into the corner where the mailbags were, that they *did* forget, and were sure to cuddle up to one another and go to sleep.

Mother Muff was quite worried, but after she learned that Postmaster Jones laughed when he saw them there, she felt better.

One morning, when Kitten Spot was finishing her after-breakfast nap and Mother Muff was attending to Kitten Gray's bath, Kitten Fluff decided to enjoy a little waltz, with her tail for a partner.

Before she knew it, she had waltzed through the open door into the post office and halfway across the room. Then she stopped short, and with a great deal of dignity, walked over to the mailbags. One of them was apart from the others, and was open a little. Kitten Fluff poked her nose inside.

Then she had a bright idea!

She would go into the bag and hide from Mother Muff. Mother Muff would think she was lost. How Mother Muff would hunt for her—and how surprised Mother Muff would be to find her inside the bag!

It was a long way to the bottom of that bag, but Kitten Fluff pushed her way in and lay down very still, hiding her nose in her paws to keep from laughing. But before long, she was asleep and dreaming of a great big mouse she was going to catch when she grew up.

All of a sudden, she started up. She thought at first that Mother Muff was about to carry her off for another scolding. But it was something much worse than that. Dozens of letters (Mother Muff had told her about those paper things) were tumbling down on top of her! She was so frightened, she couldn't move.

Then there was a terrible earthquake. The light was shut out at the top of the bag, and she heard a little click. It was quite dark, and the letters kept crowding her so!

Now Kitten Fluff didn't want to hide from Mother Muff any more, and she called for her again and again, but the leather sides of the mailbag were very thick, and no sound reached Mother Muff's ears.

What a terrible time poor Kitten Fluff had! The bag was picked up, carried a long way, and thrown down again very hard. Kitten Fluff's heart beat fast. She wished she had been a good kitten, and had obeyed her mother.

Then she heard some strange rumbling noises all around her which she could not understand at all. After a while she fell asleep, but she dreamed such a bad dream about a large dog running after her, that she was glad when she woke up.

After a long while (Kitten Fluff thought it must have been several years), the bag was moved again. She had another shaking, but then a wonderful thing happened! Somebody opened the end of the bag and she and all of the letters dropped out upon a table in a long, narrow room. For a minute she was so surprised she didn't know what to do, but the next instant she jumped down and dashed across the floor, to see if she could still use her legs.

"Great Caesar!" said one of the men.

That wasn't Kitten Fluff's name at all,

but she was too astonished to tell the man so.

Another man came up from the other end of the car—she heard the men call it a car afterward—and exclaimed, "Well, that's the oddest letter *I* ever saw!"

Then the man took her up by the nape of the neck, just as her mother always did. She liked that man very much.

"Well, I declare!" he said. "If this isn't one of those kittens I saw at the Rushtown Post Office last week! I can tell it by that odd white ring on its tail."

Kitten Fluff had never cared much for rings before, but she was very glad now that her tail had one. She told all her troubles to the man in kitten language, and he seemed to understand her.

He said something to another man about telegraphing ahead and having her sent back from Greatville. Kitten Fluff was a little worried at first, for she didn't suppose there was any way of going back except in a mailbag, but the man looked so kind that she made up her mind to trust him. She went to sleep on his overcoat that had been thrown over a chair.

At last the train stopped, and a man came to the car door with a light wooden box and a pan of milk. Kitten Fluff had almost forgotten, in her excitement, how hungry she was. She had always had lunch at ten o'clock, and now it was nearly noon, so that she really was very hungry, indeed—and milk was her favorite food.

After she had lapped up a great deal of milk, the man said, "There is no more time to spare, kitty. The train is nearly due."

He put her in the wooden box and nailed

some slats at one side. She didn't like it very much, but it was a great improvement on the mailbag. There was some writing on the top of the box, which she couldn't see, but she could see some words that said, "HANDLE WITH CARE." She wondered what it could possibly mean.

Kitten Fluff didn't have time to ask, however, because another train came up just then and she was put into one of its cars. She enjoyed the ride very much because she was near a window and could look at the scenery.

It was late in the afternoon when the train reached Rushtown, and there at the station was Mike the errand boy, whom she knew quite well. He took the wooden box, with its big label, under his arm.

"By golly!" he said. "You're a funny traveler! I always said you were the liveliest one of the lot."

What a time there was when Kitten Fluff reached the post office! The postmaster and all the clerks greeted her happily, but there was no one else half so glad to see her as Mother Muff—and no one else whom Kitten Fluff was half so glad to see!

MIRANDA AND MIRIFICUS

By ERIC PARKER

Miranda was a kitten black,
  Mirificus was white.
It was about the time of day
  When it is nearly night.
Their little ears were listening,
  Their little eyes were bright.
They waited for the dinner bell,
  And thought with all their might.

Miranda said, "Mirificus,
  When dinner time is nigh,
I wonder what is meant by 'now'
And 'soon' and 'by and by.'
But what perplexes me the most
  Is whether I am I
Or whether you are someone else.
  Can you inform me why?"

Miranda said, "If black were white
  Or red a kind of blue,
Or if you happened to be me,
  And I were sometimes you,
Or we were each some other kit
  And neither of us knew,
'Twould be a pleasant task to find
  What would be best to do."

Miranda said, "Mirificus,
  I also had a plan
To try a little waltz with you
  Before the night began.
Suppose we start now—one, two three!
  I'm sure we'll do it well."
"Excuse me," said Mirificus,
  "I hear the dinner bell!"

PUSS AND THE TURTLE

ONCE upon a time there lived a pretty little kitten. His mother was just beginning to teach him how to catch mice. So one day he stole away and went down into a cold cellar to go hunting all by himself. "I'll catch ever so many," he thought. "Six for Mother, one for Spotty, one for Dotty, one for Scramble, one for Tumble, and two for poor little Flop who never is well."

Then he sat and waited. "It is the way to begin," he thought, "and I must be very quiet, like Mother!" At this moment something stirred a pile of turnips in the corner, and the top one fell off and began to roll along the cellar floor.

Puss pounced upon it. "Good!" he exclaimed. "I've killed it—though it doesn't seem to be a mouse. How cold and peculiar it feels! I wish Scramble was with me. I guess I'll go back to Mother as soon as I've caught one real mouse."

Just then he heard a hard, thumping sound. With a start and a jump he turned quickly and saw a great big turtle creeping toward him.

"Oh, dear, I don't want to catch any mouse at all!" said Puss to himself. "I want to go back upstairs!"

Still the turtle moved toward him, nearer and nearer. "Oh, oh!" thought Puss, now afraid to move. "It's going to pounce upon me. I know it is. And if I run away, he'll catch me, sure!"

The turtle came closer.

"Go away! Go away!" cried Puss. "Don't you dare touch me!"

The turtle turned around and waddled off slowly.

"Now's my chance," cried Puss, and he jumped upon the turtle.

"The very idea of that little kitten trying to hurt my hard back!" said the turtle to himself.

And so saying, he drew his head completely into his shell so that he might have a good laugh.

"Dear me!" thought Puss in horror. "Where has his head gone to? I must have bitten it off! What will Mother say?"

And he scampered away, as fast as his legs would carry him, to tell Spotty, Dotty, Tumble, Scramble and Flop the news.

LITTLE CAT'S CHRISTMAS

By *MOLLY C. RODMAN*

IT WAS the day before Christmas and Little Cat was hungry. People were busy in their kitchens making good things to eat.

"Meow! Meow!" called Little Cat.

But in many of the houses people had their radio or television sets turned on, so they could not hear Little Cat.

Little Cat lived in an alley, but she liked people. Whenever they stopped to pet her, she did not run away or try to scratch them.

Today, however, people were hurrying down the street with big boxes under their arms and no one stopped to notice her.

Little Cat sat beneath a store window and licked one of her black-and-white paws carefully. Then she made herself as clean as possible and waited. Surely somebody would notice her now!

Everywhere she heard the same sound being made over and over by people who, instead of saying "Meow!" to each other, kept calling:

"Merry Christmas!"

Little Cat had never heard this sound before. She wondered what "Merry Christmas!" meant.

She decided to try a house on the other side of the street where a group of children were playing. Surely they would notice her.

But just as she came up to them, the children made a loud noise together and frightened her away. It sounded like:

"Jingle bells! Jingle bells! Jingle all the way!"

Little Cat had never heard anything like it before. She ran until she was too tired to run any more.

Then, right in front of her, she noticed a tall stone house that was bigger than any she had ever seen. What kind of people could live in a house like this one? Little Cat arched her small back and lifted her tired head and then crept slowly up the long wide steps. She started to meow. Then she saw that the big door was wide open. Surely there would be someone inside who would give her all she needed.

Little Cat felt very much better. She walked forward, sniffing at the door as she passed through into the darkness inside.

Little Cat could see very well in the dark, but there were no people inside.

"Meow!" cried Little Cat. But no one came.

Then she noticed something in a corner. It was a baby, asleep on some straw. How often Little Cat herself had slept on straw when she could find some, and what a warm bed it had made! And what a beautiful baby this one was!

Little Cat gently nuzzled her furry cheek against the baby's and purred softly. She would not wake him. There were some other animals near the baby. One of them looked like a cow Little Cat had seen once—though she knew cows were much bigger. And she thought the lamb might be a barking dog, but it made no noise.

Suddenly Little Cat was very tired. She decided she would take a nap beside the baby and keep warm.

But first she licked her fur once more, to make sure she was as clean as possible, and then, forgetting how hungry she was, Little Cat went quickly to sleep.

She dreamed of people who petted her over and over again, even more than she dreamed of food.

When Little Cat awoke from her cat nap, a little boy and girl were looking at her.

"It's a cat in church!" said the little boy.

"Maybe," the little girl said, "it belongs here."

Little Cat blinked her green eyes.

"Meow!" she said, very softly, too.

"A cat is what we wanted most for Christmas!" the little boy whispered to his sister. "Maybe it's for us!"

"Yes, but we can't take it unless we know for sure," said the little girl.

And they walked away, leaving her alone once again.

No one needed Little Cat! She did not even follow the children, as much as she wanted to go with them.

And then a strange thing happened. Just after Little Cat closed both eyes again, she had a feeling she was supposed to open them again right away. And when she did, there were the same two children who had left her a short time ago. Both of them were trying to pet her at once.

With them was a very tall man who lifted Little Cat out of her warm bed.

"Of course you may have the cat!" he told the children. "It does not belong to anyone. It is an alley cat!"

And suddenly Little Cat knew that she was being taken to a home she never had. She was being carried through the door in the little girl's arms and then down the long wide steps in the little boy's arms.

"We'll give you all kinds of good things to eat, Little Cat!" the boy promised, petting her on one side while the little girl petted her on the other.

Little Cat purred.

"Merry Christmas, Little Cat!" the children said as they took her inside their own warm house and gave her all she could eat and drink.

Little Cat felt very full, but it was not only because she had had enough food. Now, for the first time in her life, she had LOVE, and suddenly Little Cat knew exactly what Christmas meant!

THE ADVENTURE OF PETER AND POLLY

By H. G. DURYEE

PETER WADDLE, just fresh from a combing, with his fluffy tail fluffier than ever and a new pink bow on his new leather collar, sat on the back-yard walk.

Peter was six months old, and the most trusting Angora kitten that ever mewed to be cuddled. He loved everything and everybody, even the housemaid who shooed him out of her way twenty times in a morning. In fact, the reason for his sitting on the walk was because Hilda had just closed the door on him.

He held no hard thoughts against Hilda. He knew she would save him the best of chicken scraps and see that he had plenty of gravy, so he just sat in the sun and blinked.

All was different with another kitten named Polly Coddle. Polly Coddle could get into the same yard with Peter Waddle, but she did not belong there. She lived in a yard on the other side of a tall fence, and did not belong to any family as yet. She had a three-colored coat of fur, and wore no leather collar, nor any kind of bow. The nearest she had ever come to chicken was to smell the bones thrown away in some garbage can. She was also only six months old, and today she had come to sit in the sunshine, near Peter.

Peter noticed her as she was giving a final touch of cleaning to her bib.

"Something more to love," he thought, and started along the walk. But to his amazement this "something more" humped its back, flattened its ears, and hissed. This was so unexpected that Peter stopped in his tracks.

Thereupon Polly Coddle let her ears come back to their natural position and curled her tail calmly around her toes.

"I may be poor," was what she seemed to say, "but I'm proud, too, and I don't know that little cat."

Peter sidled round and said, "Meow!" He meant it in the friendliest way, but Polly was not used to friendliness. She got up, and with one eye on Peter, moved nearer to her own fence. Peter, mistaking this for an invitation to play, made another dash, but this time was brought up so sharply by Polly Coddle's bristling manner that he barely saved himself from a backward somersault. He stared at Polly. Polly looked back, unwinking.

Peter considered. When he wanted anything in the house, and they would not give it to him at once, he would sit up on his hind legs. He certainly wanted that three-colored kitten to play with him. Perhaps she was like the people in the house, and sitting up might make her more friendly.

He rose on his hind legs, dropped his front paws as he had been taught, and waited. Polly looked at him out of sleepy eyes, and went on with her washing.

Peter dropped to all fours again. He felt a little discouraged. There was one other thing he could do, however. He had known it to happen that he would get his own way sometimes if he rolled over. He did not especially *like* to do this—he felt so silly afterwards—but it was worth a try.

He got ready, squirmed, twisted, squirmed some more for good measure, gave a big flop, and it was done!

And whether it was the plumy tail waving aloft, as Peter went over, or whether Polly Coddle thought a kitten who could tumble like that must be nice to play with, is not certain, but no sooner had Peter righted himself than Polly drew near, put a cautious paw on the tip of Peter's tail, and allowed him to sniff noses with her. In another minute the two were rolling one another over as if they had been lifelong friends.

And then into the midst of this frolic came an interruption. Somehow, from somewhere, through the unlatched front gate or over the low front-yard fence, a dog came along. Turning the corner of the house, he caught sight of the kittens, and making a dash down the walk, was upon them before they could untwist themselves.

It was an awful moment, and Peter, who had never had to meet danger before, would have turned to run. But Polly Coddle's experiences had taught her better than that. She knew one must never run from a dog unless one was sure of getting to a tree or fence before the dog. And this time she was not sure—the trees and fences were quite far away.

Instead, she faced squarely about, braced her paws, and swelling herself up beyond anything one would have thought possible, hissed with all her might. And Peter, caught up in the spirit of defiance, swelled himself up and hissed, too.

It was a sight to stop a braver dog than this one, who not only stopped short, but backed away with a foolish bark. Upon this, Polly, humping her back higher and flattening her ears flatter, advanced sidewise. Peter, showing that he could learn rapidly, followed her example.

The dog stood perfectly still for a moment, looking at the kittens with eyes that seemed to ask if they were really in earnest, and apparently deciding that they were, gave a silly pounce on the grass, and barking at every step, as if to protest that he was not frightened, trotted around the house to the street.

Slowly the kittens unswelled themselves, and slowly but together followed to the corner of the house. Here they looked around carefully. Nothing was to be seen. All was safe and quiet.

Peter drew near Polly and bumped his head against her. Polly bumped back.

"P-r-r-t!" said Peter.

"P-r-r-t!" said Polly, which meant that they knew the danger was over, and they were very good friends indeed.

HOW SPORT SAVED THE KITTENS

ONCE, on a large farm, there was a mother cat and five little kittens. One of the kittens was gray, like its mother. Another was black with one white paw. A third was black all over. And the other two looked exactly alike.

The mother cat told her kittens to be kind and polite to everyone—and to be very kind to dogs—and each night, before going to sleep, she made them repeat these words: "Let dogs delight to bark and bite, but little kittens, never!"

One day, a big dog named Sport came to live on the farm. Sport was full of fun, and he thought that chasing cats was great fun. Five large apple trees grew near the barn in which the cat and the kittens lived, and when Sport first saw the cat family, he thought it would be fun to frighten the mother cat into the hayloft and chase each one of the five kittens up a tree.

So he barked loudly and sprang in upon the happy cat family. To his great surprise, the kittens, instead of arching their backs up to twice their size and hissing, all sat quite still and looked quietly at the stranger to see what he was going to do next.

Then there was a long pause, followed by two short paws which the gray kitten put out toward the dog, as though she would like to shake hands with him if she only knew how. This so amused Sport that he tapped the kitten very gently on the back, and then the cat, dog and kittens were soon rolling and tumbling about the barn floor in a frolic. From that moment on, Sport and the cat family were great friends.

Not many days after this, the five kittens were playing along the bank of a small river which ran behind the barn, and noticing a board which lay with one end on the ground and the other in the water, they all jumped upon it. But they were no sooner upon it than the board drifted loose from the shore and started down the stream!

The kittens were very frightened, and cried aloud for help, and though the mother cat hurried out of the barn, she could not do anything for them. She could only run up and down the bank, and she was afraid that all the kittens would be carried down to the millpond and over the dam. But suddenly she heard a familiar bark, and the next moment Sport was at her side. The dog saw what the trouble was at once, and the thought came to him that, if he would bark as loudly as he could, someone might run down to the river to see what was the matter, and then the kittens would be saved.

So Sport began at once. How he did bark!

In less than two minutes, one of the men came running toward them.

It was the farmer himself. He thought from the great noise Sport was making that the dog must have found a family of woodchucks, and so when he caught sight of the kittens he began to laugh.

But then he took a long pole, and very slowly and carefully pulled the kittens ashore. Then he picked them up in his arms and carried them toward the barn, while the mother cat and Sport walked behind.

That night, the mother cat asked her kittens what or who had saved their lives.

"Not counting you?" asked two or three kittens in one breath.

A smile lit up the face of the happy mother cat as her little ones said this, but she only said, quietly, "No—you needn't count me."

"Then," said the all-black kitten, "it must have been the farmer."

"Or the long pole," said the kitten with one white paw.

"It was Sport," cried the little gray kitten.

"We owe a great deal to Sport," said their mother, "but most of all to the fact that you have always tried to be polite and kind to everyone about you. Sport would never have come to save you if you had been ill-tempered kittens, and I hope you will always remember the lesson of this day—will you?"

"I will," said the one white-pawed black kitten.

"I will," said the all-over black kitten.

"We will remember," said the two that looked exactly alike.

"I will remem—" began the little gray kitten. But before she could finish the sentence, she was sound asleep!

KITTY AND MOUSIE

Once there was a kitty,
　　White as the snow.
In a barn he used to frolic,
　　A long time ago.

In the barn a mousie
　　Ran to and fro,
For she heard the kitty
　　A long time ago.

Two black eyes had kitty,
　　Black as a crow,
And they spied the mousie
　　A long time ago.

Four soft paws had kitty,
　　Paws soft as snow,
And they caught the mousie
　　A long time ago.

But kitty caught the mousie,
　　Mousie cried out "Oh!"
But she slipped away from kitty
　　A long time ago.

THE KITTEN THAT
FORGOT HOW TO MEW

Peggy had two brothers and three cousins, all boys, and each boy had a little dog. At first the dogs would tease Peggy's kitten, but they soon learned better. Then the dogs and the kitten played together. All day long out in the yard you could hear them saying, "Mew," and "Bow-wow-wow." But there was only one "Mew," and there were many "Bow-wow-wows." After a while the little kitten hardly ever spoke at all.

One day she wanted to say "Mew." She tried and tried and tried, but all she could say was, "M-m-m-bow," which was just as much like a dog as a kitten. She had forgotten how to do it. She was so very sad that she ran out and cried.

The Big White Hen passed by and said, "What is the matter, little kitten?"

"Oh, White Hen," said the kitten, "I have forgotten how to talk kitten talk. I try and I try and I try, and all I can say is, 'M-m-m-bow.'"

"Never mind, little kitten," said Big White Hen. "I will teach you to talk. Listen to this: 'M-m-m-cut, cut, cut, cut, ca-dak, cut!'"

"No," said the little kitten, "that is not the way to talk kitten talk."

"Well, my children learned that way," said Big White Hen, and she walked away.

The little kitten began to cry.

Along came a sheep.

"What is the matter, little kitten?"

"I have forgotten how to talk kitten talk. I try and try, and I can't," said the kitten.

"Well, never mind," said the sheep, "I will teach you to talk kitten talk. Listen: 'M-m-m-baa!'"

"No, that isn't kitten talk," said the kitten.

"Well, my lambs learned that way," said the sheep, and went on.

"What is the matter, little kitten?" said the horse, when he saw the kitten crying.

"Oh, dear me, I have forgotten how to talk kitten talk. I try and try, and I can't," said the little kitten.

"Never mind, I'll teach you to talk. Listen to this: 'M-m-m-nicker, nicker, nicker!'"

"No, no, that isn't kitten talk," said the kitten.

"Well, my colts learned that way," said the horse, and trotted off.

"What is the matter, little kitten?" said the old cow.

"I have forgotten how to talk kitten talk. I try and try, but I can't."

"Never mind," said the good cow, "I'll teach you how to talk. Listen to me: 'M-m-m-moo.'"

"No, no, no, that isn't kitten talk."

"Well, my little calves learned that way," said the cow, and she went into the field.

The little kitten saw the baby sitting near the kitchen door.

"Dear baby," she said, "I am in trouble. I have forgotten how to talk kitten talk. Can you teach me?"

The baby nodded his head and began, "M-m-m-goo, goo."

"No, that isn't kitten talk."

The kitten sat down on the doorstep, and cried and cried and cried.

"What is the matter?" said a soft voice behind her.

"Oh," sobbed the little kitten without looking up, "I have forgotten how to talk kitten talk. I try and try, and I can't—and nobody can help me. All I can say is, 'M-m-m-bow!' "

"Look at me," said the soft voice. The little kitten looked up, and there stood a beautiful big cat.

"I can teach you how to talk."

And she did. The little kitten never again forgot how to mew, although she played with the dogs every day.

JULIET'S SPECIAL VALENTINE

By MOLLY C. RODMAN

THERE were only two things in the world
that Mr. Buttercup really *liked*.
One of the things was flowers,
And the other was Juliet, his Persian cat.
Juliet had fur as white as the daisies in
Mr. Buttercup's florist shop,
And eyes as blue as larkspur.

But although Mr. Buttercup had all the flowers he wanted,
And all the *cat* he wanted,
He was not happy.
And Juliet knew why.
Not enough people came to buy flowers from him,
Because there werc only two things in the world that Mr. Buttercup liked,
And neither of the two things were
People!
And, as Juliet often tried to tell him—
If you don't like people,
People won't like you, either.
So, the few people who still came to Mr. Buttercup's to buy flowers
Only came because his shop was closer than any of the others.
But Mr. Buttercup was losing much more money than he was making,
Until he could hardly afford to pay the milkman
For Juliet's cream,
Or the butcher
For Juliet's hamburger steak,
Or the market where he bought flowers for his shop.

Juliet was worried when she saw that Mr. Buttercup

Was losing his own appetite,

Because he couldn't afford to have one any more.

If things kept getting worse,

Mr. Buttercup wouldn't be able to keep Juliet,

And somebody else would have his florist shop.

Juliet meowed sadly but softly to herself.

She didn't want Mr. Buttercup to hear how sad she felt about him.

He was sad enough already!

So when Juliet jumped in his lap after dinner,

She purred loudly, just as if

They were the richest people in the world.

If only Mr. Buttercup liked people

The way he liked flowers,

Then business would be

Very much better!

But Juliet just couldn't make Mr. Buttercup understand,

For she liked everybody.

Of course, to tell the truth, Juliet liked Mr. Buttercup

More than anybody else in the world!
Even though she would rub up against
Any person's legs
To show that she wanted to be friendly.
Juliet also liked flowers.
She often sat for hours,
Watching Mr. Buttercup make bouquets
And wreaths,
And beautiful orchid corsages.
But now he didn't have enough work
To keep him busy even half a day.

So he just sat and folded his long hands,
And looked even more worried for the rest
of the day.

If only Juliet could help him!

In a few more weeks it would be Valentine's day.

Many people would be buying flowers then
To give to the people they liked best.

Now, Mr. Buttercup was the person
Juliet liked best.

And so she wished she could give him a valentine,
Just to show how much she liked him.

But the only thing Juliet knew how to do
to flowers
Was to sniff petals and find out
How nice they smelled!

A few days before February 14th
Juliet had an idea.

Maybe she could give Mr. Buttercup a valentine after all.

Maybe!

Mr. Buttercup had spent almost his last
dollar
For a special valentine window display.

He had made a big heart
Out of red roses,

And there were silver letters across it that said:

"Won't *you* be *our* valentine?"

Juliet decided that she would be a window sitter,

So when people passed by

And saw her sitting under the heart,

They would stop and notice

What a wonderful florist Mr. Buttercup really was!

So, on the night before Valentine's day,

When Mr. Buttercup wasn't looking,

Juliet jumped in the window

And sat there very quietly, near the beautiful heart,

Waiting for morning and people.

But, long before morning came,

Something wonderful happened—

So that by the time

People started on their way to work,

Juliet was sitting proudly under the red heart

With her own valentine bouquet of half a dozen

Wee white kittens, arranged carefully around her.

Now, she was not only a window sitter,

But a baby sitter for her own new family,
as well!

Now she could give Mr. Buttercup more
than just one valentine!

For here were *six* of them!

And who could wish for any nicer bouquet
Than half a dozen cuddly little kittens?
People stopped to look in the window.
Some of them looked so long
They were late to work.
And soon there were so many people
That the people standing behind them
Couldn't see what there was in Mr. Butter-
cup's window.

Then people started coming inside the shop in crowds and ordering flowers,
And congratulating Mr. Buttercup on the valentine window display
He didn't even know he had!
"How original!" the people said.
"What an artist Mr. Buttercup is!"
And then a strange thing happened when Juliet turned to look at Mr. Buttercup.
He smiled for the first time in months,
And he kept on smiling and talking
To *people*—
Just as if he liked them!
The same way he liked flowers
Or cats!
Juliet purred loudly.
Now, everything was going to be all right.
So many people came in and ordered flowers,
That in just a few days
Mr. Buttercup had to hire somebody
To help him get corsages made.
But the very first thing he told his new helper to make
Was a beautiful orchid corsage
For his white cat, Juliet,
Who really deserved one!

THE ADVENTURES OF
BOOTS

By *GAIL STEPHENSON*

I'M THINKING about a kitten, a very new, very small, soft furry kitten. He's black all over except for his paws. His paws are white, all four of them. Because of his four white paws he is called Boots. Here he is, and very glad to meet you. "Hello, Boots!"

"Murrp!"

Boots is a very curious kitten and you know what that means. He wants to know about things. Like what's inside a paper bag. Or behind the kitchen door. He wonders what the wastebasket is like inside. Up he scrambles and holds on with his claws. He peeks over the side. OOOOOOOOPS! He finds out all of a sudden, because it tips over. And there he sits in all the papers. "Wastebaskets are fun!" says Boots to himself. "They crackle!"

Boots sniffs with his nose in the air. "I wonder what that is?" he says to himself. He sniffs again and follows his nose. All the way out to the kitchen. There is something for him in his very own dish. "Good enough to eat," he says to himself and eats it all up. Every last bit. Boots, that was fish.

"Very good fish," says Boots to himself and washes his face. Even curious kittens always wash their faces and paws after meals. Why? Because they like to be clean.

"Now I'm sleepy," says Boots to himself. "Where was that cozy place? Over this way, I think. Yes, here it is." He turns round three times on Mother's blue sweater and curls up in a tight little ball with his tail tucked under his chin. Before he finishes his second purr he is sound asleep. Even curious kittens like to take naps. And you know why. Being tired is no fun.

"Murrp!" says Boots, waking up all of a sudden. "What was that?" he says to himself, getting to his feet. "Something woke me up. I wonder what it was. Now where's my cozy place? Oh, there it goes!" Boots grabs with both paws, but the sweater gets away. Mother wants to put it on.

Boots stretches, arching his back. Way up. He almost stands on tiptoes. Then he sits down and yawns. A tremendous yawn. "What next?" he says to himself. "I guess I'll explore. I'll find out what's under here."

"Achoo!" says Boots from under the stove. "Achoo!"

Boots, that was dust. Fuzzy gray dust. Let's clean it up.

"Murrp!" says Boots, chasing the mop. "Achoo!"

"Wooooops!" says Boots, being picked up. "Meow!" he says, being hugged too tight. "It's an odd way to ride," he says to himself, his hind legs bobbing in the air. He twitches the tip of his tail because he is getting angry.

"Meow!" says Boots, landing on four feet. He shakes himself and says a few things with his tail—twitch, twitch. That means, "I don't like to be squeezed."

Boots, that was a little boy loving you. He didn't mean to hug you too tightly.

Boots walks stiffly away into the dining room. He washes himself with his little pink tongue. He washes himself where the hug was so tight. To make it feel better.

Boots sees a piece of paper tied to a string. It moves and crackles. "Now what is that?" he says to himself. "I'll chase it and find out." He runs after it and almost catches it. He hides behind a chair and waits for it. As it goes by, he jumps out and catches it. He sniffs it and pokes it with his paw. But the paper doesn't move. He likes things that move.

Scoot goes Boots. Very fast. Into the living room. He's hiding there somewhere. Not under the chair, nor behind the door. Not under the sofa, but there is a ball and a toy truck under there. Not in the wastebasket, nor behind the sewing cabinet. Where can he be? Boots, where are you?

"Murrp!"

Here he comes with a thump and a clatter! And all the books, too. Boots, what were you doing behind all those books in the bookcase? Kittens don't like stories.

Now Boots has found something that kittens *do* like. No, it isn't the paper on a string. What can it be? He's hiding it with his little white paws. He gives it a push and there it goes. And Boots goes after it. Right under the table in the dining room. He holds it with his front paws and kicks it with his hind paws. There it goes again! Now Boots is going to pounce. He crouches down, his tail straight out. His hind quarters wriggle. There he goes! Pounce! Boots has caught it!

What was it? It was his catnip mouse. Kittens like catnip. It has a special smell. Special for kittens. We can't smell it, but kittens can. It tickles their noses.

Now let's leave Boots chewing his catnip mouse. It's his favorite toy and he wants to play with it. He smells it and rolls it about all by himself.

See how busy he is! If we're very quiet, he won't even know we've gone. Let's just whisper, now, ever so softly, "Good-by, Boots!"

"Murrp!"

THE CAT AND THE FOX

A FOX was boasting to a cat one day about how clever he was. "Why, I have a whole bag of tricks," he bragged. "For instance, I know of at least a hundred different ways of escaping my enemies, the dogs."

"How remarkable!" said the cat. "As for me, I have only one trick. I wish you could teach me some of yours."

"Well, sometime when I have nothing else to do," said the fox, "I might teach you one or two of my easier ones."

Just at that moment they heard the yelping of a pack of hounds.

The cat scampered up a tree in a flash and disappeared among the leaves. "This is the trick I told you about," she called down to the fox. "It's my only one. Which trick are you going to use?"

The fox sat there trying to decide which of his many tricks he was going to use. Nearer and nearer came the hounds. When it was quite too late, the fox decided to run for it.

But even before he started, the dogs were upon him. And that was the end of the fox, bagful of tricks and all!

THE CATS' TEA PARTY

Five little pussycats, invited out to tea,
Cried, "Mother, let us go—oh, do! for good
    we'll surely be.
We'll wear our bibs and hold our things as
    you have shown us how—
Spoons in right paws, cups in left—and make
    a pretty bow;

We'll always say, 'Yes, if you please,' and
  'Only half of that.' "
"Then go, my darling children," said the
  happy mother cat.
The five little pussycats went out that night
  to tea,
Their heads were smooth and glossy, their
  tails were swinging free;

They held their things as they had learned,
  and tried to be polite—
With snowy bibs beneath their chins, they
  were a pretty sight.
But, alas for manners beautiful, and coats as
  soft as silk!
The moment that the little kits were asked
  to take some milk,

They dropped their spoons, forgot to bow, and
  —oh, what do you think?
They put their noses in the cups and all began to drink!
Yes, every naughty little kit set up a meow
  for more,
Then knocked the teacups over, and scampered through the door!